To Trevor

From: Great Grandma ☺

Christmas 2009

ANGELS IN ACTION

Helen Haidle

Illustrated by

David Haidle

THOMAS NELSON PUBLISHERS

Nashville • Atlanta • London • Vancouver

Published in Nashville, Tennessee, by Thomas Nelson, Inc., Publishers, and distributed in
Canada by Word Communications, Ltd., Richmond, British Columbia.

Scripture quotations are from The Contemporary English Version. Copyright © 1995,
American Bible Society.

Editor: Lila Empson; Copyeditor: Dimples Kellogg; Page Design: Harriette Bateman;
Packaging: Kevin Farris, Belinda Bass; Production: Kathy Profio.

ISBN 0-7852-7576-2
Printed in the United States of America.
1 2 3 4 5 6 — 01 00 99 98 97 96

In memory
of our beloved mother, Ella Winckler Beckman,
who first shared her angel experience,
prayed for this book, and is now praising her Savior
with the angelic host of heaven.
We trust that God has told her how
her prayers were answered!

With thanks
to Connie Soth for editing assistance,
to many faithful friends who prayed for this book,
to those who shared God's work in their lives,
and
to Pastors Chuck Updike, Keith Reetz, and James Muir
for their critiques.

WHO ARE ANGELS?

Our almighty God created everything, from microscopic cells to the vast universe. God also created an invisible world you cannot see—angels are part of that world (Colossians 1:15–16; Psalm 148:2–6)!

Angels are different from people. They are spirit beings. Their spirit bodies are not ordinarily seen by humans. They do not have parents because God created each one of them individually. Angels are not people who have died. They existed before any people ever did. In fact, they watched and "rejoiced" with God as he created everything on earth (Job 38:4–10).

Angels worship and serve God (Hebrews 1:6). Their desire is to obey and carry out God's commands: "All of you mighty angels, who obey God's commands, come and praise your LORD!" (Psalm 103:20).

WHAT IS GOD'S PROMISE ABOUT ANGELS?

"God will command his angels to protect you wherever you go. They will carry you in their arms, and you won't hurt your feet on the stones" (Psalm 91:11–12).

During World War II, Bill Brabham's P38 airplane flew in thick clouds as he returned to an air base in England. When his plane was over London, the flight instruments quit working. Bill's plane tipped downward in a 550 mile-per-hour nosedive.

"I was too close to the ground to bail out," said Bill. "When the plane broke out of the clouds about a hundred feet above ground, it switched directions and headed back up at a 45-degree angle! Out the left window I saw an eight-foot-tall spirit being standing calmly by my wing. His robes and golden hair were unruffled by the wind."

The instruments still didn't work, so when the plane reached a higher altitude, Bill parachuted out. "I landed in a grassy backyard—my plane crashed in another yard. No one was injured. I'm thankful my family prayed every day for me."

WOULD IT BE FUN TO SEE AN ANGEL?

Fun, yes! But it is an awesome experience! God's angels are not chubby babies with wings. They are powerful and mighty. The apostle John saw one angel whose face shone like the sun. The angel was covered with a cloud, with a rainbow over his head (Revelation 10:1).

Often when angels appeared in the Bible, their strength and blazing glory overwhelmed people. Even fearless soldiers fainted at the sight of an angel (Matthew 28:4). Daniel described one angel: "His body was like a precious stone, his face like lightning, his eyes like flaming fires, his arms and legs like polished bronze, and his voice like the roar of a crowd." When Daniel saw the angel, he "became weak and pale . . . and fell facedown" (Daniel 10:6–9). How would *you* have felt?

HOW MANY ANGELS ARE THERE?

God created more angels than you can count. Only he knows how many angels exist. If you saw God's throne in heaven, you would probably say what John said: "I heard the voices of a lot of angels around the throne. . . . There were millions and millions of them" (Revelation 5:11).

Daniel also saw God's throne and said, "Countless thousands were standing there to serve him" (Daniel 7:10).

WHO SEES ANGELS?

Most of the time, angels are closer than you think. They work unseen around you. God does not explain why some people see them and others do not.

Individuals, such as Mary, have seen one angel (Luke 1:26–27). The shepherds of Bethlehem saw a large number of angels (Luke 2:13). Sometimes people, like George Dikeman, see the *results* of an angel's work.

George and his high school buddy stopped their car at an intersection in Kansas. All of a sudden, an approaching truck turned and headed straight toward George's side of the car.

The next thing George knew, he was standing in the road. The truck had crushed the left side of his car. George's friend was alive, pinned against the seat. If George had been in the driver's seat, he would have been dead. The steering wheel was pushed into the backseat.

When help arrived, everyone asked, "How did you get out of the car without opening your door or window?" George could not answer. Neither could his buddy or the truck driver. Between seeing the truck coming at his windshield and standing unharmed in the road, George remembered nothing!

CAN ANIMALS SEE ANGELS?

A donkey once did! Balaam, the donkey's owner, was traveling to meet the king of Moab. The donkey ran off the road—for a good reason. An angel with a sword blocked the way! Balaam did not see the angel. He beat his donkey, forcing it back on the road. That happened two more times.

Then God let the donkey talk. It said, "What have I done to you that made you beat me three times? . . . You've ridden me many times. Have I ever done anything like this before?"

God let Balaam see the angel, too. The angel scolded Balaam, saying, "You had no right to treat your donkey like that! . . . If your donkey had not seen me and stopped . . . , I would have killed you and let the donkey live."

Balaam was sorry. The angel let him continue on his journey but warned him to say only what God told him (Numbers 22:21–35).

Do animals today see angels? A beautiful Balinese cat named Cashmere lay on Judy's lap. The cat lifted her head toward the doorway. Judy looked up, too, and saw a tall white-robed angel enter the room. Judy glanced back at her cat. *Does Cashmere really see the angel, too?* she wondered. As Judy watched, her cat's eyes followed the angel's every move!

HAS ANYONE SEEN ANGELS MORE THAN ONCE?

Isaac's son, Jacob, did. He left home because his brother threatened to kill him. When night came, Jacob lay down to sleep. In his dream, angels went up and down a stairway that reached into heaven. God spoke from the top of the stairs, promising to bless all nations through Jacob, and to bring him back home someday (Genesis 28—32).

Years later, an angel told Jacob in another dream to return home. As Jacob traveled home, "some of God's angels came and met him." When Jacob saw all the angels, he was amazed and said, "This is God's camp" (Genesis 32:2). On the night before Jacob was reunited with his brother, a stranger wrestled with him. The prophet Hosea said that the stranger was the Angel of the Lord (Hosea 12:2–4).

HOW STRONG ARE ANGELS?

No human power compares to the power of an angel. Yet angels possess only a fraction of God's almighty power. One angel rolled away the stone weighing thousands of pounds at Jesus' grave. Another angel destroyed 185,000 enemy soldiers who surrounded the city of Jerusalem (2 Kings 19:35).

Before Paul and Patti left on their trip, they asked God to guard their travels. As they were driving through a major intersection, a speeding sports car approached from the left and ran the red light. Paul related, "It came toward us at such a high speed, I knew a collision was unavoidable! At that moment, a large white-robed figure intercepted the sports car, bringing it to a complete stop a few feet from us. We stared in amazement as the powerful figure looked back into our car as if to make sure we were all right, then disappeared.

"God definitely sent a mighty angel to intervene," Paul said. "And we continued on our trip, praising God and rejoicing in his goodness!"

WHAT DO ANGELS DO?

"Angels are merely spirits sent to serve people who are going to be saved" (Hebrews 1:14). Angels do not live inside you. They work around you, behind the scenes, as God's secret agents. If you saw how much they do in your life, you would be amazed! God assigns angels to help and serve you today as they helped others, like Elijah, in the past.

When Queen Jezebel decided to kill Elijah, God's prophet, he escaped to the wilderness. As he lay sleeping, an angel touched him and said, "Get up and eat."

In front of Elijah lay a jar of water and loaf of freshly baked bread. He ate and went back to sleep. Later the angel woke him again, saying, "Get up and eat, or else you'll get too tired to travel." Elijah obeyed. That food gave him strength to walk forty days (1 Kings 19:1–9)!

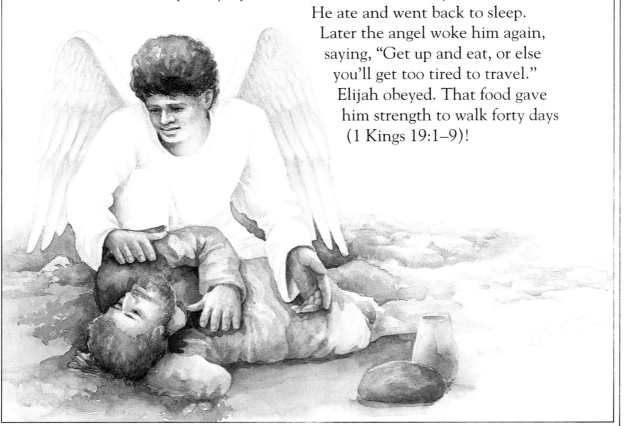

HOW DO ANGELS SERVE US?

During World War II, Allen Simantel and other American troops were captured in Europe. "They forced us to march 100 miles, in snow and subzero temperatures, to a prison camp. We received only two meals all week," said Allen.

"One snowy evening, as we trudged along, I glanced up. A beautiful little girl stood beside the road. In the dusk, her bright eyes smiled at me. She acted like she knew me as she walked toward me and lifted up her covered basket. When she pulled back the white shawl, I saw six small biscuits. I was so hungry! I reached for the biscuits and stuffed them in my pockets. The girl flashed a radiant smile as she turned to leave.

"I was dumbfounded! The other men didn't seem to notice her. If they'd seen the biscuits, they would have fought over them—everyone was starved!

"I can still see her face," Allen says today. "It shone so clearly and brightly in the dusk. No mother would have let an eight-year-old girl take food to enemy troops at night. I believe she was God's angel!"

WOULD YOU RECOGNIZE AN ANGEL?

Angels sometimes appear in disguise. God tells us, "Be sure to welcome strangers into your home. By doing this, some people have welcomed angels as guests, without even knowing it" (Hebrews 13:2).

That happened to Abraham. Three men walked, talked, and ate with him. They were actually God and two angels in disguise (Genesis 18:1–33).

Later, God sent the two disguised angels to the city of Sodom. Abraham's nephew, Lot, invited them to stay at his house. The angels told Lot about their mission to destroy the evil city. In the morning, the angels hurried Lot and his family out of town, saying, "Run for your lives! Don't even look back. And don't stop in the valley. Run to the hills, where you will be safe." After Lot and his family left, burning sulphur fell from the sky, destroying Sodom (Genesis 19:1–29).

DO ANGELS HAVE WINGS?

The Bible describes angels as moving through the sky, but it does not usually mention whether or not they fly with wings. Angels seen by the shepherds came down from heaven and went back up (Luke 2:8–15). John saw an angel "flying across the sky" (Revelation 14:6). Gabriel "came flying in" to Daniel (Daniel 9:21).

The prophet Ezekiel saw many-winged "living creatures" around God's throne (Ezekiel 1, 10). The prophet Isaiah had a vision of "flaming creatures with six wings each. . . . They covered their faces with two of their wings and their bodies with two more." With their other two wings, they flew over God's throne, loudly praising God (Isaiah 6:1–4).

HOW DOES GOD USE ANGELS TO ANSWER PRAYERS?

If you honor the LORD, his angel will protect you" (Psalm 34:7). King Herod arrested Peter and assigned sixteen soldiers to guard him. The night before his trial, Peter was asleep, chained between two guards. An angel woke him, saying, "Quick! Get up!"

Peter wondered if he was dreaming. His chains fell off and he followed the angel past the guards. The front gate swung open, and the angel led Peter down the street and suddenly disappeared. Peter could hardly believe it! "The Lord sent his angel to rescue me from Herod!" he exclaimed. Then Peter ran to a friend's house where he found many people praying. God's angel had been sent to answer their prayers (Acts 12:1–19).

DOES GOD STILL USE ANGELS TO ANSWER PRAYERS?

Judy listened intently to the newscast. American troops planned to invade Iraq at any moment. Her son, a marine, would be one of the first into action. "Lord, you know where Jeff is," she prayed. "Please send a hedge of angels to guard him." A picture flashed in Judy's mind—Jeff lay on a sandy hill, holding his rifle. His guardian angel stood behind him. Then six more angels arrived and surrounded him like a hedge.

After the invasion, Jeff phoned and said, "Mom, I knew you prayed for me before the war began. I couldn't see them, but I felt angels all around me!"

WHAT IS GOD'S "SPECIAL DELIVERY" SERVICE?

God speaks to us through his Word, the Bible. But sometimes he uses "special delivery" service—angels! The word *angel* means "messenger." God's angels go only where he sends them and say what he tells them. Their appearance is usually unexpected. Angels do not hang around— they deliver God's message, then disappear. Angels expect prompt obedience, even though they may not explain everything.

The *first* person in the Bible who heard an angel messenger was Hagar, a servant of Abraham. She ran away into the wilderness, but the angel of the Lord found her and said, "Go back" (Genesis 16:9–11). Hagar obeyed.

God also used angel messengers to give directions to Abraham (Genesis 22:11–18), Elijah (2 Kings 1:1–17), Philip (Acts 8:26–40), and Cornelius, a captain in the Roman army (Acts 10:1–33).

Cornelius was fasting and praying when an angel in bright clothes appeared. The angel said, "God has heard your prayers and knows about your gifts to the poor. Now send some men to Joppa for a man named Simon Peter. He is visiting with Simon the leather maker, who lives in a house near the sea."

Cornelius sent his men to Joppa. When they brought Peter back, he told Cornelius the good news of God's love and forgiveness in Jesus. Everyone in the house was filled with God's Spirit and they were all baptized in the name of Jesus.

Do Angel Messages Encourage Us?

A fierce storm pounded the ship carrying the apostle Paul to Rome. Everyone gave up all hope of survival. But during the night, an angel brought God's message to Paul. The next morning, Paul told the 276 people on the ship, "Cheer up, because you will be safe. Only the ship will be lost. . . . Last night [God] sent an angel to tell me, 'Paul, don't be afraid! . . . Because of you, God will save the lives of everyone on the ship'" (Acts 27:21–26).

The ship fell apart in the storm, but everyone grabbed planks and floated to the island of Malta. No one was lost, just as the angel had said.

DO ANGELS STILL BRING GOD'S ENCOURAGEMENT?

Ella Beckman cried as she got out the empty packing boxes. She dreaded moving. Suddenly a strong, warm hand gripped hers. Someone unseen stood beside her. Ella squeezed the unseen hand. *It's real—it's not just my imagination!* she thought. The hand led her to the boxes. As she walked, she heard the swish of invisible clothing.

If God wants me to pack, it must be okay to move, Ella realized. While she packed, the hand held hers. And when she finished, the hand vanished.

Later she read God's promise: "I am the LORD your God. I am holding your hand, so don't be afraid. I am here to help you" (Isaiah 41:13).

21

DOES EVERYONE BELIEVE AN ANGEL'S MESSAGE?

Most people in the Bible believed God's messengers. Once, Gideon had trouble believing what the angel of the Lord told him. But he did obey God's message and won a great victory over the Midianite army (Judges 6—7).

The priest, Zechariah, could not believe at all when an angel told him, "Don't be afraid, Zechariah! God has heard your prayers. Your wife Elizabeth will have a son." Zechariah knew that he and his wife were too old to have children.

Then the angel said, "I am Gabriel, God's servant, and I was sent to tell you this good news. You have not believed. . . . So you will not be able to say a thing until all this happens." And Zechariah was unable to speak until after his son's birth (Luke 1:9–20)!

ARE ANGELS HARMED BY FIRE?

Flames of fire are your servants" (Psalm 104:4).

Sometimes angels appeared in or with fire. But they never seemed to be harmed by it.

While Moses tended a flock of sheep, the angel of the Lord appeared in a burning bush. Moses saw the bush on fire, but it was not burning up. So he went closer to see it. God spoke to Moses and sent him to lead the Israelites out of Egypt (Exodus 3:1–10).

Gideon prepared an offering of meat, bread, and a pot of broth for the angel of the Lord who spoke to him. When the angel touched the food with a staff, flames leaped up, consuming the food—and the angel vanished (Judges 6:11–24).

Manoah's wife was childless. An angel told her she would have a special baby. She ran and told her husband, who asked God to let the messenger reappear. The angel returned and gave them instructions about their child. Manoah prepared a burnt offering, and the angel rose up to heaven in the flames (Judges 13:1–24).

CAN ANGELS RESCUE PEOPLE FROM FIRE?

King Nebuchadnezzar built a huge gold statue and commanded everyone to fall down and worship it. Three young Jewish men refused to bow down to anything besides God. The furious king told his soldiers to tie up the three men and throw them in a hot furnace.

Suddenly the king jumped up and shouted, "Weren't only three men tied up and thrown into the fire? . . . I see four men walking around. . . . None of them is tied up or harmed, and the fourth one looks like a god" (Daniel 3:24–25).

The king ordered them to come out. Their clothes did not smell like smoke and not one hair on their heads was burned! The king proclaimed, "Praise their God for sending an angel to rescue his servants!" (Daniel 3:1–29).

DO ANGELS RIDE IN FLAMING CHARIOTS?

One morning Elisha's servant looked out the window and saw an army of horses and chariots surrounding the city. The Syrian king had sent his best troops to arrest Elisha. "Sir, what are we going to do?" the servant asked Elisha.

Elisha said, "Don't be afraid." He saw something no one else could see—on the hills surrounding the city was an even bigger heavenly army! He told his servant, "There are more troops on our side than on theirs." Then Elisha prayed, "LORD, please help him to see."

"And the LORD let the servant see that the hill was covered with fiery horses and flaming chariots."

What "troops" did Elisha see? Were angels in the fiery chariots like an angel was in the burning bush Moses saw? We do know that God blinded the Syrians, and their plan to capture Elisha failed (2 Kings 6:8–23).

DO ANGELS RESCUE PEOPLE?

God's angels protect and rescue his people during danger. When Moses brought God's people out of Egypt, the Egyptian army attacked from the rear. An angel moved behind the Israelites, shielding them from attack (Exodus 14:19).

Because Daniel would not stop praying to God, he was arrested and thrown into a den full of hungry lions. The king worried all night and rushed to the den early the next morning. To his surprise, he heard Daniel call, "My God knew that I was innocent, and he sent an angel to keep the lions from eating me" (Daniel 6:21).

DO ANGELS STILL RESCUE PEOPLE?

Five young cousins hauled buckets of water into the Canadian prairie. While two boys dumped water down gopher holes, the other boys waited with nets. Flushed out of their underground burrows, gophers ran everywhere. When the empty-handed boys stopped to catch their breath, they looked up to see a snorting bull angrily pawing the dirt. The boys took off running! But coming over a ridge, they were stopped short by wire fencing. The barbed wire was too close to break through or crawl under.

"O God, help us!" they screamed. Instantly the boys stood on the other side of the fence, staring in amazement at the furious bull! There was no explanation for their rescue . . . not one scratch was found on any of them. Had God's angels performed the impossible feat?

WHO IS GOD'S CHIEF ANGEL?

Only two angels are named in the Bible: Michael and Gabriel. Michael is called "the chief angel" (Jude 9). The apostle John described "Michael and his angels" fighting the devil and his angels (Revelation 12:7–9). Because he is chief angel, Michael's shout will announce Jesus' return to earth someday (1 Thessalonians 4:16).

Once when a messenger angel tried to deliver God's word to Daniel, evil forces held him back for twenty-one days. That angel told Daniel, "Then Michael, . . . one of the strongest guardian angels, came to rescue me" (Daniel 10:13). The angel continued, "Michael, the chief of the angels, is the protector of your people" (Daniel 12:1).

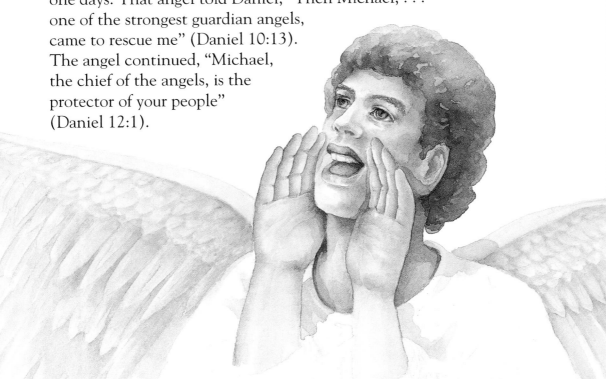

DO ANGELS PROTECT US TODAY?

One of God's powerful angels saved Judy Harris of Portland, Oregon, from certain death. "The light turned green and I drove out into the intersection," she said. "A sports car from the other side drove out, too. I glanced to my left, as something caught my eye. Speeding down Canyon Road, a driverless delivery truck barreled toward me!"

Judy screamed, "Jesus!" and braced for the deadly crash.

"Instantly the truck was on the other side of my car!" she said. "It swerved across the road and hit a telephone pole where it stopped. I didn't understand! How could that truck pass between our two cars in the intersection? There was no room!"

Judy laughed and said, "I'll never forget the astonished look on the other driver's face! I, too, felt amazed. Then God let me see a big angel sitting on the hood of my car!"

DOES GOD HAVE A SPECIAL AMBASSADOR?

Twice the angel named Gabriel appeared to Daniel, bringing God's wisdom in answer to Daniel's prayers (Daniel 8:15–26; 9:20–27). God also used Gabriel to announce the coming of Jesus, first to Zechariah, then to Mary (Luke 1:17, 31). Gabriel told Mary, "You are truly blessed! . . . Don't be afraid! . . . You will have a son. His name will be Jesus."

Mary wondered how that could happen. Gabriel explained, "The Holy Spirit will come down to you, and God's power will come over you." Gabriel told Mary that her older cousin, Elizabeth, was also going to have a baby. Gabriel said, "Nothing is impossible for God!" And Mary believed Gabriel's message (Luke 1:26–38).

WHAT DO ANGELS USUALLY SAY?

When angels first appear, they often tell us not to be afraid. Shepherds were frightened when an angel appeared in the brightness of God's glory. The angel said, "Don't be afraid! I have good news. . . . A Savior was born for you. He is Christ the Lord. You will know who he is, because you will find him dressed in baby clothes and lying on a bed of hay."

Suddenly many angels filled the sky, praising God and saying, "Praise God in heaven! Peace on earth to everyone who pleases God." After the angels left, the shepherds hurried to Bethlehem and found Jesus, as the angel said (Luke 2:8–16).

WHERE ARE ANGELS WHEN YOU ARE AFRAID?

When young Joyce Rose lived in Tucson, she watched out for scorpions and black widow spiders. But snakes scared her the most. And she just knew snakes hid under her bed. Each night, she was afraid to walk to her bed after turning off her light on the wall. So every night, after she flipped the switch, she would run and leap into the safety of her bed!

One dark night, Joyce woke up, frightened. A glowing figure stood by her door. She knew it was an angel. Its presence calmed her. "Seeing God's angel comforted me when I was ten years old," Joyce says today. "I never saw the angel again, but I always *knew* it was there. And I no longer feared snakes under my bed."

DID ANGELS EVER HELP SAVE JESUS?

Joseph of Nazareth took Mary to be his wife after an angel appeared in his dream and said that her baby was "from the Holy Spirit." The angel told Joseph to name the baby Jesus (Matthew 1:18–25).

After Jesus was born, an angel spoke to Joseph in another dream: "Get up! Hurry and take the child and his mother to Egypt! Stay there until I tell you to return, because Herod is looking for the child and wants to kill him." Joseph left immediately with Mary and Jesus. Later, the angel directed Joseph in two dreams to return home (Matthew 2:13–22).

WHAT DID JESUS SAY ABOUT ANGELS?

Jesus called a child over to him and said, "Don't be cruel to any of these little ones! I promise you that their angels are always with my Father in heaven" (Matthew 18:10, 14).

Each child is very precious to God. Angels pay close attention to God's orders regarding children. You can trust God's promise that one or many of his angels are nearby, ready to help you.

Peg visited a family in Portland, Oregon, one evening. When she peeked in the baby's room, she saw a bright angel standing at the head of little Sarah's crib. Peg said, "The angel glanced up at me, nodded slightly, then turned its full attention back to the baby."

Will You Be an Angel in Heaven?

God made you a very special person. You will always be yourself. In heaven, you will be more like angels in some ways—you will not get married or die, but you won't turn into an angel. Jesus said, "In the future world no one . . . will either marry or die. They will be like the angels and will be God's children, because *they* have been raised to life" (Luke 20:35–36, emphasis added).

Will Jesus Tell Angels About You?

Do not be embarrassed to tell others by your words and actions that Jesus is your Savior. Jesus promised, "If you tell others that you belong to me, [I] will tell God's angels that you are my followers" (Luke 12:8; Revelation 3:5).

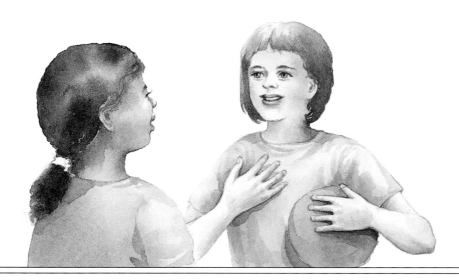

DID JESUS EVER NEED THE HELP OF ANGELS?

Although Jesus was the Son of God, he was also human. His body got tired and hungry, especially once when he spent forty days without food. At that time, the devil tried to trick Jesus. He took Jesus on top of the temple and said, "If you are God's Son, jump off. The Scriptures say: 'God will give his angels orders about you. They will catch you in their arms, and you won't hurt your feet on the stones.'"

Jesus refused. It was not right to test God like that. After Jesus resisted all temptations, the devil left. Then God sent angels to help and strengthen Jesus (Matthew 4:1–11; Mark 1:12–13).

DO ANGELS STILL HELP US?

Ann, a missionary teacher, took a bus trip to several churches in Canada. She planned to sleep overnight in one bus depot. When she arrived, she found out that the depot would be locked during the night.

Another woman, whom she had not seen before, walked up and asked, "You don't have anywhere to sleep, do you?"

Ann shook her head. "No."

"Come with me—there's a hotel nearby," invited the woman. Ann followed and wondered, *I feel like this woman knows all about me! But how will I pay for a room?*

At the hotel, the stranger paid for a room with two beds. Ann lay down on one bed and fell fast asleep. After only a few hours of sleep, the women rushed back to the depot to catch the morning bus. "I checked my bag," Ann explained. "Then I turned to thank my new friend, but I couldn't find her anywhere! Did I share a room with an angel?"

COULD ANGELS HAVE RESCUED JESUS?

The second time an angel helped Jesus was in the Garden of Gethsemane. Sweat, like great drops of blood, fell from Jesus' forehead as he prayed, "Father, . . . please don't make me suffer. . . . But do what you want, and not what I want." God did not save his Son from suffering, but he did send an angel to strengthen Jesus (Luke 22:39–44).

When Jesus finished praying, soldiers arrived. Peter pulled out his sword to fight! But Jesus said, "Put your sword away. . . . Don't you know that I could ask my Father, and right away he would send me more than twelve armies of angels?" (Matthew 26:52–53). (One army numbered about 6,000 soldiers. Twelve armies would number 72,000! But Jesus did not ask his heavenly Father to send angels to rescue him. He chose to suffer and die on the cross so we could have eternal life.)

WHAT IS THE BEST ANGEL MESSAGE?

On Friday, after Jesus died, his friends buried him in a tomb that had been cut into solid rock. They placed a heavy stone in front of the entrance. Sunday morning, a great earthquake struck. An angel from heaven, whose face and clothing shone like lightning, rolled away the huge stone. Roman soldiers, who guarded the tomb, shook with fear— then fainted!

Later, some women, bringing burial spices for Jesus' body, went inside the open tomb. Two men, gleaming like lightning, appeared and said, "Why are you looking in the place of the dead for someone who is alive? Jesus isn't here! He has been raised from death" (Luke 24:5–6; see also Matthew 27:62—28:4).

WHAT IS THE NEXT BEST ANGEL MESSAGE?

During the forty days after his resurrection, Jesus appeared to many people. One day he took his disciples outside the city. As he blessed them, Jesus rose up in the air and disappeared in a cloud. While the disciples stood there staring up, two men in white clothes appeared and said, "Why are you . . . looking up into the sky? Jesus has been taken to heaven. But he will come back in the same way that you have seen him go" (Acts 1:11).

Angels want people to hear the good news of Jesus. Angels said to the women at the tomb, "Go and tell his disciples, and especially Peter" (Mark 16:7). And later, when religious leaders imprisoned the disciples for preaching about Jesus, an angel led them out of jail and said, "Go to the temple and tell the people everything about this new life" (Acts 5:20).

WHAT SIGNAL DO ANGELS WAIT FOR?

Angels wait for "the sound of a loud trumpet" when God will tell them to bring everybody who believes in Jesus to heaven. When will this trumpet blow? Nobody knows, not even the angels (Matthew 24:36). But the Bible says we will hear it when Jesus comes "on the clouds of heaven with power and great glory." Just as angels announced his birth, proclaimed his resurrection, and explained his ascension, angels will accompany Jesus when he returns (Matthew 24:27–31).

SHOULD YOU WORSHIP ANGELS?

Angels in the Bible urge us to praise God as they do. This is one angel's message: "Worship and honor God! . . . Kneel down before the one who created heaven and earth" (Revelation 14:7). No matter how beautiful or powerful angels may be, worship belongs only to God (Colossians 2:18).

Once a mighty angel showed the apostle John a new heaven and a new earth (Revelation 21). John bowed to worship at the angel's feet, but the angel stopped him immediately and said, "Don't do that! I am a servant, just like you. I am the same as a follower or a prophet or anyone else who obeys what is written in this book. God is the one you should worship" (Revelation 22:9).

SHOULD YOU PRAY TO ANGELS?

God says, "Pray to me in time of trouble. I will rescue you" (Psalm 50:15). People in the Bible prayed directly to God. No one prayed to angels or called on them for help. Angels are responsible to God and under *his* orders.

Manoah asked God to send the angel messenger (Judges 13:8).

Even Jesus did not ask angels for help. Once Jesus told his disciples that he could ask his heavenly Father to send thousands of angels to help him (Matthew 26:53).

Many people prayed to God for Peter, and God sent an angel rescuer (Acts 12). Your job is to ask God for help. He has promised to hear your prayers. Angels are one way God answers prayer. "God will command his angels to protect you" (Psalm 91:11).

WHERE ARE ANGELS WHEN BAD THINGS HAPPEN?

God does not explain why he lets bad things happen. He does tell us that he can make bad things turn out for *good* in our lives. When troubles come, it does not mean God is angry with you or has forgotten you. You can be sure God loves you, no matter what happens. God and his angels stay close to you, especially when things go wrong.

In 1982, eight-year-old Scot Law's mother died in a car accident. Scot's father was out of town, so the Roberts family took him home. When Scot went to bed, he cried for hours. "About 2:00 A.M., Mrs. Roberts came into my room," said Scot. "She sat on the edge of my bed and prayed. She asked God to help me and to send his ministering angels to give me peace."

Scot continued, "After she left the bedroom, I noticed a tall, bright figure in the corner of the room. At first I thought I was dreaming. I blinked my eyes a couple of times, but it didn't go away—it was an *angel*! It glowed, like when you see a light through a fogged-up window. The angel's arms stretched toward me and I felt peaceful.

"I knew my mother was with God in heaven, and that God was watching over me—everything would be okay. I kept awake as long as I could, watching the angel. It stayed there until I fell asleep."

Angels did not rescue Jesus from the cross. They did not stop the king from throwing Daniel in the lions' den. Angels may not rescue you from a problem, but they will be close by to strengthen you *during* trouble as they helped Daniel and Jesus.

WHAT MAKES ANGELS HAPPY?

Angels aren't robots. They have feelings and emotions, just like you do. Angels rejoice, worship, celebrate, and even shout. Can you imagine what it sounded like when "morning stars sang, and angels rejoiced" (Job 38:7)?

When a billion angels praise God, it gets noisy! "Shout praises to the LORD! Shout the LORD's praises in the highest heavens. All of you angels, and all who serve him above, come and offer praise" (Psalm 148:1–2).

But do you know what angels like best, besides praising and serving God? When someone asks Jesus to be his or her Savior, angels cheer! Jesus said, "God's angels are happy when even one person turns to him" (Luke 15:10).

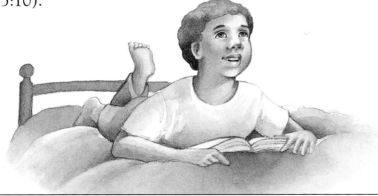

ARE ANGELS WITH US WHEN WE DIE?

Jesus told about a poor, sick beggar who died and was carried by an angel to God's wonderful home (Luke 16:19–22). Jesus promised to prepare a special home in heaven for you (John 14:2–3). It is "the city of the living God, where thousands and thousands of angels have come to celebrate. Here you will find all of God's dearest children, whose names are written in heaven" (Hebrews 12:22–23).

Eight-year-old Katie was dying of leukemia. Every day her parents stayed with her at the hospital. Finally, she could not sit up in bed or lift her head anymore. One afternoon Katie was asleep. Suddenly she sat straight up in bed with her eyes wide open. She laughed as she stretched her arms up high. "Oh! It's Jesus and his angels!" she said to her mom and dad. Then Katie lay back on her pillow and peacefully died. Katie's parents miss her, but they will never forget her joy when Jesus and his angels came to take her to heaven!

WHEN WILL YOU GET TO SEE ANGELS?

God could open your eyes at any time to see the angel beside you. But you can still trust God, even if you never see an angel here on earth. (Remember: You may have already seen one . . . in disguise.) Someday, in heaven, you will see God and his angels. And you will find out the special times angels helped you during your life. You will be so surprised. You will jump up and down for joy! And together with millions of angels, you'll thank God for his great love and for the ministry of his angels. Perhaps they will even show you around your new home. It is going to be *grrrreat!*